THE AMAZING SPIDER-MAN 2

SPIDER-MAN vs. ELECTRO

ADAPTED BY BRITTANY CANDAU

BASED ON THE SCREENPLAY BY ALEX KURTZMAN & ROBERTO ORCI & JEFF PINKNER

PRODUCED BY AVI ARAD AND MATT TOLMACH

DIRECTED BY MARC WEBB

ILLUSTRATED BY ANDY SMITH, DREW GERACI, AND PETE PANTAZIS

MARVEL

NEW YORK • LOS ANGELES

© MARVEL marvelkids.com © 2014 CPII

All rights reserved. Published by Marvel Press, an imprint of Disney Book Group. No part
of this book may be reproduced or transmitted in any form or by any means, electronic or
mechanical, including photocopying, recording, or by any information storage and retrieval
system, without written permission from the publisher. For information address Marvel Press,
1101 Flower Street, Glendale, California 91201.

Printed in the United States of America

First Edition

3 5 7 9 10 8 6 4 2

Library of Congress Control Number: 2013955171

G658-7729-4-14105

ISBN 978-1-4847-0536-0

SUSTAINABLE
FORESTRY
INITIATIVE

Certified Chain of Custody
Promoting Sustainable Forestry

www.sfiprogram.org
SFI-01415

The SFI label applies to the text stock

THERE WERE PLENTY OF NORMAL THINGS Peter Parker could have been doing right then: hanging out with his girlfriend, Gwen Stacy; building gadgets in Aunt May's garage; or, probably most importantly, attending his high school graduation. But Peter wasn't exactly normal. Nope, he had a secret identity as the Super Hero Spider-Man. And though it wasn't easy, and though every week the *Daily Bugle* printed stories calling the masked hero a menace, at this very moment, duty called.

Spidey swung from car to car, catching up to the criminal Aleksei Sytsevich, who was speeding around in a stolen truck.

"Can't we just cut to the part where you start to cry and give up?" Spidey, hanging casually off the side of the van, asked Aleksei.

SPOOKED by the web-slinger, Aleksei swerved. He hit a taxi, launching it into the air. And it headed straight toward a bespectacled man holding an armful of blueprints.

In one swift motion, Spider-Man shot a web to a nearby lamppost and carried the man to safety.

"You're Spider-Man!" the man cried out excitedly. Spider-Man was his hero. He couldn't believe this was happening. Usually no one even noticed him.

"Nice to meet you, Max," Spider-Man replied, eyeing the Oscorp badge on Max's shirt. Max beamed. Spider-Man knew his name!

A FEW MONTHS LATER, Max ran into Gwen. She worked at Oscorp, too. As they chatted in the elevator, Gwen learned that Max had come up with lots of interesting ideas for saving electricity.

"Hydropower is so cool! That was you?"

Max sighed bitterly. "Yes, not that anyone would know it." He looked up at the TV and saw Spider-Man swing across the screen. "It must be nice to have everyone . . . the whole world see you like that."

Little did he know that soon enough . . . it would.

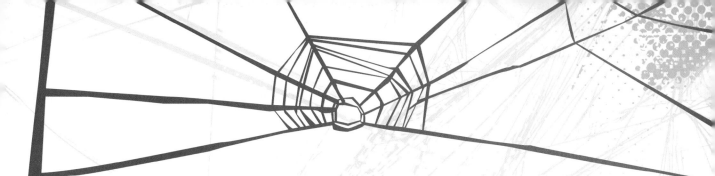

ONE NIGHT, Max stayed at work long after everyone else had gone home. There was a problem in the lab that needed to be addressed right away.

Max grumbled to himself as he set up his tools. "'Max, make sure everything's working.' 'Max, fix this.' 'Max, fix that.'"

He trudged up the stairs to the top of the water tank, which glowed brightly from the electric eels swimming around in it. Opening the system, he found a loose wire sticking out.

"AHHHHHH!" As soon as he reconnected the wire, the system's power surged and shocked Max. Losing his balance, he fell right into the tank!

MAX WOKE UP a few hours later in a strange room. He had no idea where he was or how he got there. He felt so . . . strange. He stumbled outside and found himself being drawn to the bright flashing lights of Times Square.

A loud HONK made him turn. He was in the middle of the street . . . right in the path of a delivery truck! He threw his hands up and electric bolts shot out, making the truck flip and slide across the road.

Whoa. Had those come from him? He looked down and saw his hands were glowing. Moments later, police officers, fire trucks, helicopters, and news crews flooded the scene. People were looking at him. People seemed to fear him.

And he liked it.

ACROSS TOWN, Peter felt his spider-sense tingle. Something was happening in Times Square. He quickly changed into his suit and swung across the cityscape.

When he arrived, he saw a glowing figure surrounded by officers. Arcs of electricity wildly flew off him, dangerously close to shooting into the TKTS bleachers where dozens of tourists sat. The whole scene was magnified and projected on the huge jumbotrons surrounding Times Square. Spidey walked toward the man, telling the officers to hold their fire.

As he got closer, Spider-Man recognized the glowing figure causing all the fuss. Max— the guy with the blueprints! He had no idea what had happened to this guy, but he knew he had to calm him down somehow. Before Max . . . or somebody else got hurt.

"Hey! Max! You're one of the good guys. I don't think you want to be here," Spider-Man said, slowly walking toward him.

"I want people to notice me," Max replied simply.

"They are," Spider-Man said, gesturing to all the jumbotrons displaying Max's face.

AT THAT MOMENT, the jumbotrons flashed, and Spider-Man became the one projected on all the screens. Max broke out of his awed stupor. Anger coursed through him. He started firing electric bolts out of his hands.

"Stop! Max, people are going to get hurt!" Spider-Man yelled.

"You can call me Electro now," the glowing figure replied, thinking that the name was rather fitting. He was a new man now. A new, powerful man.

He continued to shoot the electric arcs and finished his thought. "Maybe they deserve to get hurt."

"Wrong choice, Max," Spider-Man said.

Spider-Man flung a web at Electro, trying to stop the villain in his tracks. But something strange happened. The web conducted electricity back to its source, and zapped Spider-Man. Hard.

SPIDEY WAS FLUNG BACKWARD, right into a cop car.
Dazed, he looked at his wrist. Electro's surge had fried one of his web-shooters. But he
still had one good one left.

He sprang up to see Electro firing blasts into the air and hitting a towering building.
Debris crumbled down, rapidly heading toward the people below. Spidey swung down
and rescued a man who was about to be hit from the debris.

Spider-Man webbed the man away using his good web-shooter. As the jumbotrons
showed Spidey carrying the man to safety, the crowd cheered and started chanting,
"Spidey! Spidey! Spidey!"

ELECTRO'S FACE clouded at the sound. How dare Spider-Man betray him like this! He used to be his hero. But he was just like the rest of them. Selfish.

In a blind rage, Electro hurled a nearby car straight toward the crowd still on the bleachers.

Spider-Man jumped into action, using his one web-shooter to stop the car midair. Of course, this only elevated Electro's fury.

The vengeful villain slammed his hands down in anger and electricity surged all around him. This was going to be a fight!

ELECTRO CHARGED at Spider-Man, ready to shock him again. Thinking quickly, Spidey webbed a fire hydrant, swinging it around just as one of Electro's power blasts hit him. Spidey doubled over, losing his grip on the web. The hydrant hurtled right into Electro, smashing him into a jumbotron. The screen exploded in a shower of sparks.

But Electro didn't feel hurt. In fact, he just felt thirsty . . . for more power. He started soaking up the electricity from a loose wire. All of a sudden he floated in the air, a crazed look in his eye.

He uses power to regenerate, Spidey thought in awe as Electro started laughing maniacally from his perch above.

A PLAN started to formulate in Spider-Man's mind. What didn't mix well with electricity? Being a science geek really had its advantages sometimes.

Meanwhile, Electro surveyed the scene beneath him. The chaos, the fear-stricken people…it was beautiful. I made this happen, he thought proudly.

WHHOOOOOOOSHHHH.

Suddenly, a blast of water hit the levitating villain. Wearing a fireman's hat, Spider-Man, along with two firemen, directed a large hose at Electro. He started to short out like a wet lamp and crashed to the ground. He was still trembling as guards from the Ravencroft Institute for the Criminally Insane loaded him into their van.

Spider-Man watched the scene sadly. Of course, Electro needed to be put away before he caused any more harm. But he'd started out as Max. And Max had been a nice guy, right?

SPIDER-MAN thought more as he swung across the city. However he had gotten those powers, it was Max's choice how he used them. And though Spidey knew more than most how difficult it could be to be different, he also knew that he had a responsibility to use his abilities to help the people who needed it.

Spidey swung deeper into the brisk night. He'd chosen to be the web-slinging, friendly neighborhood Spider-Man. And he wouldn't have it any other way.

$4.99 US / $5.50 CAN

WHEN THE AMAZING SPIDER-MAN hears that a Super Villain is terrorizing Times Square, he swoops into action! Arriving on the scene, Spidey finds a man in a hood pulsing with blue energy: **ELECTRO!** Now, with hundreds of innocent bystanders in harm's way and endless energy at Electro's fingertips, will the wall-crawler be able to stop New York City's newest menace? Or will he be zapped like a bug?

ISBN 978-1484705-36-0

50499

9 781484 705360

EAN

The Legend of
PINKFOOT

When you see a ⭐, hold the book up to a light source for 30 seconds. Then turn off the lights to see the pages glow. The glow-in-the-dark stickers work the same way—and add to the fun!